/15
xile: _____

/BL: _____

Points: _____

# Oh Brother!

## Growing Up with a
## Special Needs Sibling

written by Natalie Hale
illustrated by Kate Sternberg

MAGINATION PRESS • WASHINGTON, DC

*To Kelly, fellow traveler and parent extraordinaire.*
*I couldn't do it without you. — NH*

*"Wheels on, wheels off!"*
*With love to my big little brother Frank Sklarsky, who still loves cars. — KS*

Published by
M A G I N A T I O N  P R E S S
American Psychological Association
750 First Street, NE
Washington, DC 20002

For more information about our books, including a complete catalog, please write to us,
call 1-800-374-2721, or visit our website at www.maginationpress.com.

Editor: Darcie Conner Johnston
Art Director: Susan K. White
The text type is Sabon
Printed by Phoenix Color

Library of Congress Cataloging-in-Publication Data

Hale, Natalie.
Oh brother! : growing up with a special needs sibling / by Natalie Hale ;
illustrated by Kate Sternberg.
p.    cm.
Summary: An eleven-year-old girl finds ways to handle the unique challenges
presented by her thirteen-year-old mentally disabled brother by looking for his
good qualities and taking the rest in stride.
ISBN 1-59147-060-9 (hardcover : alk. paper) —
ISBN 1-59147-061-7 (paperback : alk. paper)
1. Children with disabilities—Family relationships—Juvenile literature.
2. Brothers and sisters—Juvenile literature.
[1. People with disabilities. 2. Brothers and sisters.]
I. Sternberg, Kate, 1954- ill. II. Title.
HQ773.6.H25 2003
306.875'3—dc22                                                    2003011671

Manufactured in the United States of America
10  9  8  7  6  5  4  3  2  1

# Contents

Dear Reader,

Having brothers and sisters has its ups and downs, no matter what. They can be our best friends, sharing our secrets, making us laugh, or helping us with our homework. When they're younger, they can be cute and oh-so-easy to love. But there are times when they are a pain, too! Getting angry or frustrated with siblings is just a normal part of family life.

If sisters or brothers get sick, getting along with them can be harder than usual, because they need a lot of your parents' attention until they get well again. And when a sister or brother has a condition that isn't ever going to go away, it can be much harder. Lots of kids have a sibling with what we often call "special needs." "Special needs" is a general term that includes Down Syndrome, Attention-Deficit/Hyperactivity Disorder, autism, cerebral palsy, Asperger Syndrome, and just about any other developmental or physical disability.

When kids have a sibling with any of these special needs, they face more difficult challenges every day. For example, parents usually have to give more of their time and energy to a child with disabilities, while the "typical" siblings feel neglected. Sometimes kids feel they have to be another parent to their special needs sibling and can't be a kid themselves. They might feel sad, or angry, or embarrassed about their sibling's behavior or appearance. They might be teased for having a brother or sister who is called "weird"—or worse. They worry about having children of their own. And they can feel isolated from classmates and friends because their family is "different."

If you are one of these kids, this book is for you.

It's a true story about 13-year-old Jonathan, who has special needs, and his younger sister Rebecca, who does not. Like you, Becca has coped with all of the problems and worries listed here, plus a few more. Told by her, *Oh Brother!* is honest. It doesn't sugar-coat the feelings and struggles that she faces every day. And most important of all, it is full of real-life, kid-tested suggestions for dealing with those situations.

I hope that Becca's experiences will give you ideas, make you laugh, and lighten your life. And I wish the greatest happiness to you and your special family.

Sincerely,
Natalie Hale

# CHAPTER 1

# Send Him to Mars

"Can't Jonathan go live somewhere else? China, maybe. Or Mars. I hear Mars is nice."

I was studying the planets in science class, and the thought of sending my brother to Mars sounded like a great idea.

Mom set down her book. I noticed it was called *Cosmos*. Maybe she was studying about Mars, too, and didn't think it was such a great idea.

"Becca, what's bothering you, hon?" she said.

I groaned. "Jonathan's driving me crazy."

Mom looked at me like she was waiting for me to say more.

"I used to be able to understand him better than anyone, but now his words sound like he is from China or Mars. It's so hard to try to understand him, and sometimes I'm just too *tired* to try. He talks about the same things over and over. He's always taking my stuff out of my room. And he's so rude when I walk into his room. He just yells, 'Lemme alone! Go away!' Then later he wants to be best friends again like nothing happened!"

"I see," said Mom.

I threw myself across the sofa. "We were best friends. We used to have so much fun. Then he got to be thirteen and I got to be eleven, and everything changed."

"Bec," said Mom, "is this the same boy who gives us bear hugs and makes us laugh with his jokes? The same guy who works so hard at chores that he makes the rest of us look like we're standing still? That brother?"

I knew she was reminding me of Jonathan's good points to try to put me in a good mood, but it wasn't working. I was still upset. So I kept going.

"My friends have normal brothers. When I play at Laura's house, I think, why can't I have brothers like Lee and Eric? Why couldn't Jonathan be just a regular, ordinary person? Big brothers are supposed to be nice to their little sisters."

"I know," said Mom.

"So...how about Mars?" I asked cheerfully.

She laughed.

I scooped up Lilly, my calico, and snuggled into the sofa. "You understand, don't you, girl?" I murmured.

"Purrrrrrr," she answered, like she always does.

Mom sat down beside us. She tickled Lilly's chin while she thought a minute. Then she said, "Maybe it's time to consult a pro. A real pro, someone with day-in and day-out solutions."

Oh, brother! I groaned to myself. Don't we have enough special education pros for Jonathan? "Like who?" I grumbled.

Mom smiled. "Like you."

"Me???"

"I've watched how you handle problems with Jonathan," said Mom. "You've figured out more solutions than anyone I know. Maybe you just forget to use ideas that you've already thought of. Talk to yourself about it. You might be surprised at what you find out."

"I don't know," I said. "Maybe."

I believe cats can smile, and Lilly smiled at me right then. Purrrrrr.

# CHAPTER 2

# Laughing

Okay. I'm talking to myself about it.

"Becca, don't let Jon's behavior bother you," says Dad. "Just let it zip right over your head." He says he learned to let lots of things zip right over his head in life, and that's why he's going bald, from all those things passing over his head. I think he made up that last part. But I get what he's saying.

Maybe one way I get along with my brother is by seeing that some of the things he does are just really funny. It's almost like he's trying to entertain us on purpose. Which he probably is, because he's got a great sense of humor. The more I laugh, the more it lightens me up.

When Jonathan was younger (like five or six or seven) and did something naughty, sometimes Mom or Dad would put him in a chair for time out. After one or two minutes, he'd get bored and want to go play his drums in his room. Of course he couldn't, since he was in time out.

So he came up with the perfect solution: He grabbed the chair, stuck it to his bottom, and tiptoed back to his room hunched over like a furniture mover. Then he'd start banging away on his drums. As if Mom wasn't going to hear him!

Then there's the Fire Alarm Story.

At school Jonathan's gym teacher asked him to do some exercises in a spot right next to the wall. On that wall was a funny-looking red handle with the words, "Emergency. Pull down." His special ed teacher had been talking about emergencies all week, teaching the class what an emergency means and what to do when you're in one.

I guess Jonathan wasn't interested in doing the class exercises and was sitting there looking around for something to do. I can picture the whole thing. He noticed the red handle on the wall. He noticed the writing. Words! Gym seemed boring, but words were fun. Jonathan was a good reader. So he read.

"Emergency." Yeah, I know that word. "Pull down." Okay, I can do that.

YANK!

I was in the middle of a fractions assignment when the fire alarms started blasting and the school went crazy. We were pretty happy about hurrying outside with all the kids and teachers, and we hoped the fire would get our math books before the fire trucks that were screaming down the street could put it out. But of course there was no fire. It was my brother, who is now famous at Jacobs Middle School, just doing a good job of reading!

9

Jonathan also has a great ear for music. He loves musical instruments and has tons of music books all over his room. He studies them and knows more about instruments of the orchestra than anyone I know, except my dad, who is a music professor.

One night, we were eating supper when Jonathan's bottom accidentally made a loud and embarrassing noise. I was waiting for him to say, "Excuse me," like Mom and Dad taught him, but he didn't. He cocked his head and thought for a minute. We all looked at him and waited.

Then he said, "Sounds like a bass clarinet."

After everyone could actually breathe again from laughing so hard, my mom said, "How about a double bassoon?"

"Nope," said Jonathan. "Bass clarinet."

My dad, the other music expert in the family said, "I think the man's right."

Then there's the Smoke Story. When Jonathan was eight, he loved smoke. He wanted to know where it came from and what made it. He saw steam coming from the clothes dryer vent, and he asked, "Smoke?"

"No, Jonathan. Not smoke. Steam," said Mom.

He noticed steam rising from a pot cooking spaghetti, and he asked, "Smoke?"

"No, Bud," Dad would say. "Steam."

When Mom put powder on him during hot, sweaty weather, he saw the puffs of powder in the air and asked, "Smoke?"

"Not smoke, my friend. Powder," said Mom.

One day, Jonathan was playing in his room, and he got very quiet. Mom always said that was a bad sign. But she was busy, so it was a while before she checked on him. When she finally did, I heard a scream like from a horror movie and came running to see what was up. Oh, brother! The room was totally white. Jonathan was sitting on the floor with a huge shaker of baby powder, shaking it up and down and filling the air with "smoke." The whole room was caked with powder—the floor, the bed, the lamps, the books and toys, even the ceiling fan.

It looked like it had snowed inside.

Poor Mom was totally speechless. Maybe she was thinking about the zillion hours of vacuuming that she'd have to do. But I also bet she was glad that Jonathan didn't use any matches for his "smoke experiment"!

Only *half* a zillion hours later (I helped clean up), Mom and I collapsed on the sofa. "One day," she said, "this will be funny." She opened one eye and looked at me. Then we both burst out laughing.

# CHAPTER 3

# Protecting My Space

I learned the hard way that it's my job to protect
my room and to make sure Jonathan doesn't take
my things or ruin them. I try to remember that he's
like a little kid and doesn't understand some rights
and wrongs yet.

Jonathan would just go into my room when I
wasn't there and take what he wanted, like my CDs,
or my books, or the pictures of me and my best
friends hanging on my wall. If a picture has a pretty
girl in it, Jonathan wants it hanging in his room.
Once he even took my favorite Broadway poster
because he thought it was "spectacular." (That was
his favorite new word at the time.) He tried to tack
it up on his own wall, but it wouldn't stick. When
he got frustrated, he crumpled it up and stuffed it
under his bed!

Sometimes he would just come into my room and
wreck something or break something or make a big
mess. Once I was writing an essay on my computer
and left my room for one lousy minute, and
Jonathan came in to play a computer game, closed
my essay, and lost the whole thing.

Another time, he knocked a big plant off my
bookshelf. Number one, the plant was in this great
pot that Dad got once when he was in Mexico, and
it broke. Number two, it broke all over my math
homework on the floor and ruined it. Number three,
he tried to use my best shirt to clean it up. And

number four, he left muddy footprints all the way to his room!

It used to make me so mad. I'd yell at him and try to teach him words like "trespassing" and "stealing." But then I got it that Jonathan just can't understand. If he sees something in my room that he likes, he thinks it's okay to take it. If he wants to come in and check things out when I'm not there, he thinks that's okay, too.

One time I tried to make him understand by doing to him what he'd done to me, like the Golden Rule, only in reverse. When he took my CDs, I took all of his CDs and kept them until he missed them. Then he had to come ask me to get them back. When he did ask, "CDs back?" he seemed so humble that I thought, "Cool. He really understands what it's like now." I was so happy. I gave them all back to him and asked him if he wanted to work on our favorite jigsaw puzzle. But the next week, he took my CDs again!

"Two wrongs don't make a right," said Dad. Whatever.

Then he and Mom had a brilliant idea. They must have decided that it might be a long time before Jonathan learned to leave my stuff alone. So they called a locksmith to put a lock on my door.

Dad said, "Becca, here's your key. It's up to you to keep your room locked so that you can keep your things safe."

This works great. Except when I forget. Sometimes it seems like a whole lot of trouble to keep it locked, and sometimes Jonathan can be really good about leaving my things alone for a long time, so I don't bother. But even if I forget sometimes and Jonathan comes in, it still feels good to know that I have control over what happens in my room. It's up to me.

# CHAPTER 4

# Is It Sad?

Sometimes when I look at my brother, I feel really sad. Sometimes I even have to look away and pretend not to care because I feel so sad I can hardly stand to think about it. There are so many things he'll never be able to do and so many things he'll never understand.

When I feel really sad, I talk to myself about it. I've thought about Jonathan and what it's like for him, and I've wondered, is Jonathan sad? He likes school and his friends there, and he also can't wait to get home every day so he can play his music, dance, and make his own tape recordings. He is happy for hours and hours doing that. Ever since the day Dad called Jonathan a "recording engineer," that's what he calls himself too, and he is really proud of it.

He spends hours every day in his room taping CD music and radio music and cassette music and even video soundtracks. He knows exactly what music or movie dialogue is on each of his bezillion special tapes, and where one bit of music will start and where another one is going to stop. It's amazing. And he's always making new tapes. Mom and Dad started buying huge packages of them so that he never runs out.

Sometimes he can do things most people can't do. For instance, he can remember music if he hears it even once. We found that out last summer. Every summer my dad works in a town that has a music festival all summer long. We've been spending summers there since we were babies, and we go to all the concerts. One night when a string quartet started playing a piece, Jonathan tugged on Dad's sleeve and told him the quartet had played that same piece a few years before. Dad couldn't believe that Jonathan could have that kind of memory, so later he asked the violin player about it. The man got a shocked look on his face and said, "We played that piece here five years ago!"

Sometimes I wonder if Jonathan has a secret little world that he lives in, a world that makes him happy. I know that music must be a big part of that world. He listens to everything—rap, opera, rock, jazz, and classical music. And if he's not recording it, he's dancing around his room. And Jonathan doesn't walk. He runs, and does a little hop-skip in the air when he's especially happy. So I guess he's not sad about his disability. But I am sometimes. And I guess that's okay, too.

CHAPTER 5

# Hey! What About Me?

Dad says I figured out how to get attention the minute I was born. He says that for the first year I cried unless Mom was holding me. But by the time I was a year old, I figured out better ways to get attention.

It's not always easy to get attention. Having a special needs sibling sometimes feels like you're sitting on the family sidelines just watching the show. Mom and Dad have to spend a lot of extra time teaching Jonathan how to do things and take care of himself. Sometimes they also have to spend a lot of time solving problems that happen when Jonathan makes a mistake. Like the time Jonathan forgot he turned on the bathtub faucet and water rained through the kitchen ceiling!

I kind of disappear for a while when things like that happen. They have to give all their attention to Jonathan, and usually I can't help. It used to really bother me that they spent so much time helping him. I thought, What about me? Am I invisible?

It bothered my parents, too, so we talked about it. They could tell I was jealous, and Mom said it was important for us to find a way to spend more time together. (Dad said he didn't want me to "fall through the cracks.") Now the three of us sometimes go out to dinner while Jonathan stays home with a sitter. But that's not very often. The really big change is that every week I have special time out with just Mom or just Dad. It works out great.

When the weekend comes, Jonathan loves to say to me, "I have idea! You and Mom, girls' night out." Then he turns to Dad and grins. "Buddy date!" He means that when Mom and I go out for some special time, they stay home and have supper together and watch a video. It's Jonathan's favorite way to spend an evening, and Dad gets to put his feet up and relax. Everybody's happy.

When I'm out with my dad or my mom, it's

much easier to talk without being interrupted, and we always do something fun. Because my dad is a music professor, we get to go to lots of performances. We see music theater and ballet and concerts. Dad knows how much I love dance and music. Since he does too, we have a great time together, and I learn more about performing each time.

I have so much to talk about with my mom that I practically never stop talking when it's just the two of us. So when we're having special time together, I tell her about my friends, homework, dance class, what I want to do for summer vacation...everything. We have a favorite Italian restaurant that we go to, and Mom always lets me order dessert!

The special times alone with Mom or Dad have made it so much easier for me to handle the times when Jonathan needs all their attention. It's easier for me to understand and just be patient. He needs them too, and I know my time will come.

# CHAPTER 6

# Before You Come to My House

Okay. So I complain about my brother. I'm his sister, and that's what siblings do, right? But no one else is allowed to complain about him! One thing that reminds me that I love Jonathan is when someone gripes about him or, even worse, makes fun of him. I think, "How dare they say that! He's my brother!"

Once when I was little, I brought a new school friend home to play. After she met Jonathan, she made a mean face and said, "Why is your brother so weird?" I was so mad. I decided right then that I didn't want her for a friend, and I never asked her over again.

That's when I found out that it's better to tell a new friend about Jonathan ahead of time. I watch to see how they look or what they say when I tell them. Sometimes I can tell right away that they'll be fine with Jonathan. Sometimes I can't.

If I make new friends and they haven't met Jonathan yet, I'm always a little nervous about asking them over, and I wait a while before I do. What will they think when they meet him? Will they see any of the good things about him, or will they just think he's strange? Will they understand his jokes—or anything he says? Will they try to listen to him? Most of all, will we still be friends after they meet him? Will I want to be?

My best friends are great with Jonathan. They accept him. Maybe part of the reason they're my best friends is that they're the kind of friends who do understand and they don't look down on Jonathan because he's different.

One of my friends said, "Jonathan's cool. He says honest stuff that I want to say but can't." Another friend said, "It's awesome how Jon can remember kids' names after hearing them just once. I'm terrible at remembering names."

When I hear my friends talk like that, it makes me think about Jonathan in a new way. There are good things about him that I don't even notice sometimes. And even if he doesn't realize it, he helps me figure out who my real friends are.

If my best friends like Jonathan and accept Jonathan, and a new friend doesn't, I know we probably won't get along. And when I hear my best friends admiring Jonathan in spite of his disabilities, it also makes me feel relaxed, like all the parts of my life fit together just right.

# CHAPTER 7

# Will It Happen to Me?

"What's going to happen when I have kids?"
Mom was sitting on my bed saying goodnight. Next
to our special times out, bedtime is the best time to
talk to her about what's on my mind.

"What's going on in there?" she asked and patted
the top of my head.

"Am I going to have a baby like Jonathan? Doesn't Dad have two disabled uncles? And don't you have some cousins who are disabled?"

Mom laughed. "No, Becca," she said. "Dad's uncles are twins. They don't have disabilities. And no, I don't have any disabled cousins."

"Oh," I said. "I guess I was just thinking scared. I couldn't remember exactly. But I see how hard it is to take care of Jonathan, and I get scared. I don't think I could do it."

"That must be a scary thought for you," she said. "But you're a child, and children don't have to take care of babies, with or without disabilities. It'll be a long, long time before you're a mom."

"But Mom, someday I *will* be grown up. What's going to happen then?"

She gave me a hug. "Some kinds of disabilities run in families," she said, "and some don't. If the same disability happens again and again in one family, that means it's inherited. The disability can be passed down from grandparent to parent to child. But if a disability pops up in anyone, anywhere, with no pattern, then it's called random."

"But what makes it pop up at all?"

"Sometimes it's caused by something outside of the parents. There can be lots of reasons. Maybe the mother is exposed to something that can cause a disability while she is carrying the baby—something like a drug or a germ or too much alcohol. But many disabilities are genetic."

"Ge-what?"

"Genetic. Genetic means that the disability is

carried in the genes of a person."

"Jeans? Like blue jeans?"

Mom laughed. "Genes like g-e-n-e-s. Genes are like a set of instructions in our bodies that make each of us who we are. They make us look like ourselves, for example. They tell us whether our skin will be brown, our hair will be red or black or blond, or whether we'll be short or tall. Whether you'll have a good ear for music, or freckles, or maybe fast feet for tap dancing."

I smiled. I've got those last two.

"Okay," said Mom. "Are you ready for a test?"

I pulled my blanket over my head. She knows I hate tests.

"Here's the question," she said. "If I tell you that Jonathan's disability is genetic and random, what does that mean to you?"

"It means that Jonathan puts on his blue jeans and walks randomly around the house?" I pretended to be innocent.

"Very funny," said Mom. "You get one more chance."

"Okay, okay," I said. "Does it mean that Jonathan's disability is in his genes, and that it might or might not happen to my children, but probably not?"

"A-plus!" said Mom. "Exactly right." Then she said, "I'll tell you a story."

"Okay," I said and snuggled deeper under the covers.

"One night long ago, before you and Jonathan were born, I was watching a movie on TV. It was

about a mom and her little boy who was disabled. The mom was strong and the child was adorable, but I felt uncomfortable."

"Why?"

"Because disabilities seemed sad to me. I didn't know what to say or how to act. I couldn't even enjoy watching a good movie about it."

"So what did you do?"

"I couldn't seem to turn it off. I just kept watching that mother and child. When the movie was over, I said to myself, 'I could never do that.'"

Mom looked me straight in the eye. "But you know what? Even though I thought I could never be like the woman in the story, the moment Jonathan was born I discovered something. When a mother holds her baby, she falls in love. Dads do too, and that love gives parents the strength to do whatever they need to do. If Jonathan had been born with green skin and purple hair, we would have loved him just the same."

"*Mo-om*, there are kids in my school today who have purple hair and green skin on purpose."

She laughed. "You know what I mean. And you'll feel the same way about your children when you grow up. Whether they are shy or noisy, make bad choices or good ones, you're going to love each one in a special way."

"Oh, Mom, I don't know." I said. I felt all sad and confused inside. "I love Jonathan and I don't really want to send him to Mars even though I say I do. But I still can't believe that I could handle it if I had a baby like him. What if I couldn't? What kind

of a mom couldn't handle her own baby?"

"Honey, that wouldn't make you a bad person,"
Mom said softly. "Only you know what you can
handle and what you can't handle. There are lots of
people who can help. And there are even lots of
wonderful people in this world who want to adopt
children with special needs."

"Really?" I couldn't believe it.

"Really," she said.

When she turned off my light, I lay looking
through my window, up to the stars. Maybe everything will work out fine, I thought. Maybe I'll never
have a baby with special needs. And even if I do,
maybe everything will still work out okay. I snuggled
down into my bed. Maybe...maybe...oh, maybe I'll
just quit worrying about it!

# CHAPTER 8

# Take a Break

"Wow, Mom, you are so patient with Jonathan. How do you do it?"

The only times I've ever heard my mom yell usually have something to do with my brother. Like when Jonathan filled his room with "smoke" or when he tried to make his dinosaur collection disappear down the toilet.

"It's not always easy," she said, "and it helps to take a break. I go for a walk or call one of my friends or maybe I just sit in the sun and relax. Or Dad and I go out. Then I have a better attitude when I come back, and I can usually be more patient."

I take breaks, too. If I start snapping at Jonathan, then I know I need one. I'm lucky that Mom and Dad really listen to me when I say, "I need some space!" They help me get the space, whether it's an overnight at Laura's house, or a trip to the mall, or a few hours playing at home while Jonathan goes out with Mom or Dad.

Also, I like finding things to do on my own that are fun and exciting, things that I can do no matter what's happening with my brother and my family. I've tried different things. I sang in my church choir and got a part in "Fiddler on the Roof" at school. I joined the drama club. I wrote a poem for my school magazine. I even tried out for soccer last year. Then I found out that I love to dance! Now I take dance classes almost every day. I think about it and read about it and have new friends who love to dance just as much as I do.

So when I get home from dance class or the mall or whatever, and I see Jonathan leaping around the room to one of his tapes, I feel happy instead of crabby. Sometimes I even want to join in his fun. "Come on, Buddy," I'll say, "let's go work on our jigsaw puzzle."

And after a break, I don't mind the things he does that can make me crazy at other times. (Or at least I don't mind as much.) For instance, every day he likes to rehearse who's who and what's what in our family. So if I've had a break and he asks me for the gazillionth time, "You the daughter, right? And I the son?" it's a lot more fun to say, "You're exactly right, Buddy. I'm the daughter. And you're the son. You got it right." That always makes him happy. And I feel pretty good too.

# CHAPTER 9

# Getting My Feelings Out

If getting some space doesn't help, I know a few more tricks. Once when I was really little I got furious with my brother because he took my doll and broke it. I was so angry that I wanted to yell out all my bad feelings, but I was too young to know the words. Mom knew that I was upset and brought me some paper and crayons. "Here, Becca," she said. "Show me how mad you are."

I grabbed a fat red crayon and rubbed it hard into the paper. I drew a red girl with big red streaks coming out from her body like angry lightning.

"This is me," I said.

"Wow," said Mom.

Then she gave me another piece of paper and asked, "Now can you draw a picture of our whole family?"

I drew a big stick figure. "That's me," I said. Then I drew a smaller one. "That's you, Mommy." Then a slightly smaller one. "And that's Daddy." Then way up in the corner of the paper I drew a teensy-weensy speck.

"What's that?" asked Mom.

"That's Jonathan." It felt good to make my brother almost invisible. When I finished the drawing, it felt like all the hot air inside me had whooshed out of my body, and I smiled at Mom. I thought about my brother saying, "I sorry, Becky-Boo," and I wasn't so mad at him anymore.

"I want to draw another picture." This time I

took lots of crayons and drew a girl dancing outside in the sunshine. I drew trees and birds and yellow sunrays. "This is me, too," I said. "Can I go outside and play?"

Mom kissed me. "Let's go."

I still like to draw what I'm feeling. Now that I'm older and have words for my feelings, I write in a journal, too. Writing gives me one more way to get my feelings out. Putting my feelings on paper says, "Yes! This is what I feel!" I can look right at it. It's real.

Sometimes I write down whatever I'm feeling, and it just rushes out of me. Other times I want to think and take my time. Whenever something important has happened to me, I write about that. I want to remember it forever, and if I write it down I can read about it over and over. Sometimes I write a poem, or I copy a poem or a song that means a lot to me or says what I'm feeling.

When I'm sad or angry about something, writing helps me think things through and feel better about them or come up with answers. Sometimes I write a letter to someone in my journal if I am angry at them. I get all of my feelings out, but of course I don't send the letter to the person! It's for my eyes only, just to help me think. No matter how angry I am, I always feel better after I write a journal-letter, and I can usually talk to the person a lot more calmly and maybe even see their side of things a little better.

I think everyone has thoughts and feelings that they wouldn't want to tell anyone else because

they'd be too shy or embarrassed or even feel like a jerk. But writing in my journal helps the most when I'm completely honest, so that's what I try to do. I also try not to worry about what anyone would think if they found my journal and read it. To make sure that doesn't happen, I keep my journal in a special place where only I will see it. It's for my eyes only.

# CHAPTER 10

# Thinking Like a Genius

Sometimes a kid with a special needs brother or sister gets to practice thinking like a genius. I mean, sometimes we see a problem that no one else has been able to solve, and we think of a new solution ourselves.

For instance, no matter how many times we explain some things to Jonathan, he still can't understand them. And sometimes he makes up his mind about something and he won't change it, no matter how wrong he is. If the sun is shining but Jonathan says it's raining, then to him it's raining. These are the kinds of problems that I like trying to fix the most. Usually what it takes is having a special understanding with Jonathan.

Lots of times Dad has a special understanding with him.

They do this guy talk thing. If Dad tells him it's time to do chores, Jonathan will say, "No. I play whole day. Got it?"

Dad will say, "No, Buddy. It's chore time. Got it?"

"No way! I play whole day, Buddy-Dude."

"Don't be a pooka-snooka!"

"I not pooka-snooka! You a booga-booga man!"

By this time, they're both laughing at their made-up words, and Jonathan is going off to do his chores.

Sometimes I have a special way of understanding him, too. Like one night at supper when Jonathan was eight or nine, I got to practice thinking like a genius. We had just sat down to macaroni and cheese. It's my favorite dinner. Suddenly Jonathan jumped out of his chair and yelled, "Crumbs! Crumbs on chair! Hurt!"

I looked at his chair. "Jonathan, there aren't any crumbs on your chair. See?" The chair looked clean to me, but sometimes Jonathan feels things with his skin that we can't see with our eyes. His skin is super-sensitive, and the slightest little crumb can drive him nuts.

"Yes crumbs!" he cried. "Mom brush off!"

Mom was trying to teach Jonathan to do things for himself, so she said, "Jonathan, you don't need Mom to do it. You can brush them off all by yourself. That's something you can do."

He threw himself on the carpet. "No!" he howled. "Bad mood is here."

Well, it was no fun eating my macaroni and cheese with Jonathan crying on the floor, and I was starting to get really annoyed. Then I got an idea. What if I did just what he was doing? If he saw what he looked like, would he do something different? What would happen?

BOOM! I threw myself on the floor and started hollering with Jonathan. He bolted straight up like he'd been poked with a pin. "No!" he ordered me. "Stand up! Eat your supper."

"I will if you will," I said.

"I can't!" he howled. "Bad mood still here."

My plan had only made things worse. I had to think of something else.

"Hey!" I said. "Let's brush the crumbs off our chairs together. Okay, Jonathan?"

His face lit up. "Okay!" he said.

We hopped up and made a big fuss of brushing invisible crumbs from our chairs. Soon we were both laughing our heads off.

"Good mood is here!" Jonathan announced.

The rest of the meal went fine, and my macaroni and cheese was still warm.

# CHAPTER 11

# I'm Not the Parent

"Becca!" Mom yelled up the stairs. "Stop hovering over Jonathan. You're not the parent!" She must have heard me in his room, doing what's against the rules: bossing Jonathan around.

Mom had five younger brothers and sisters, and when she was still only ten or eleven years old she sometimes had to take care of them all by herself. She had to be a kid-parent, and she doesn't want me to be one. She and Dad say they want me to be a kid while I can still be a kid.

Okay. That's fine with me. I know that when I'm a grownup, things might be different. One day maybe I'll take over more responsibility for Jonathan. But that's a long way off. Right now my job is to be a kid.

But I really like helping him. When we were little and he was still learning how to talk, I helped him with that. There were lots of sounds he couldn't pronounce, like *S*. If the *S* came at the end of a word,

he would suck it in like he was whistling backwards. My parents and Jonathan's speech therapist worked with him all the time. And I would help too, even though I could barely pronounce his name. "Toy-*zuh*, Jon-tin!" I'd say. "Ball-*zuh*! Train-*zuh*!" And Jonathan would try to say the words like I did.

Mom and Dad loved that, but they didn't want me to go overboard. So I learned not to do things for Jonathan when he needed to learn to do them himself. And I'm still trying to learn not to worry about him or boss him around so much.

I did used to wonder if I could take care of him if I ever had to, though. And I found out. When I was old enough to babysit the kids next door, Mom got that look in her eye, that "boy-have-I-got-a-great-idea-but-you-might-not-like-it" look.

"Yeah?" I said cautiously.

"Becca, how would you feel about babysitting—kidsitting—for Jonathan? We'd pay you the same as we pay a regular sitter, and we can see how it works."

Visions of a new purple leotard and ballet CDs floated in front of my eyes, and I thought about it for half a mini-second. "Okay!"

On my first night kidsitting Jonathan, I felt very grown-up. The little sister was playing the big sister tonight. "Okay, Buddy," I said after I locked the door behind Mom and Dad. "I'll get your supper for you. Are you hungry?"

"Sure, Becky-Boo!"

Supper went fine, and then he started to watch one of his favorite videos while I cleaned up our dishes. So far, so good. Good mood was here. But after a few minutes, I came back to join him—and yikes! There were spots of blood on his hands, and on his shirt, too.

"Buddy!" I ran to the couch. "What'd you do? Did you hurt yourself?"

"No," he said. "I fine." He always says that, no matter what's wrong. But he was hiding one hand behind his back.

"Let me see your hand. Did you cut it on that video box?" I noticed a corner of the box was cracked and sharp.

"No. I fine," he insisted.

I took his hand. "C'mon, Buddy. It's just a little cut. Let's go clean you up." Usually it was so hard to get Jonathan to budge when he was watching a video. Would he listen to me?

"Oooo—kay," he sighed, and followed me like he was the little brother and I really was the big sister. I could have hugged him!

When Mom and Dad got home, Jonathan ran to the door. "Becky-Boo help me! She fix my hand!" He was so proud of me, like I had done something really special.

Maybe I'm not the parent and I don't have to take care of Jonathan every day. But I can be a really good kidsitter for my big brother.

# Nobody Knows What It's Like

"None of my friends have a brother like Jonathan," I told Dad one day. "They don't know what it's like. I told Sarah that it drives me bonkers when I hear Jonathan watching the same scene from *The Wizard of Oz* over and over again—maybe a hundred times. I told her I can't stand that movie any more, and I used to love it."

"And what did Sarah say?" asked Dad.

"She said, 'I don't know why that drives you nuts. I'd think it would make you like it even more.' I was so mad! What a dumb thing to say."

"I bet if Sarah had to listen to that scene a hundred times, she'd feel the same way you do," said Dad.

"That's what I think. She has no idea what it's like."

"You know what?" said Dad. "I know of some kids who do know what it's like."

"What do you mean?" I said. "Who? Where?"

"Right here in our city," said Dad. "There are groups of kids who get together to have fun and talk about how it feels to have a brother or sister like Jonathan. I did a search on the internet for "handicapped sibling support groups," and I found tons of information. More than we'd ever need."

"Really?"

"Sure," said Dad. "Let me know if you want to go to a sibling meeting."

So I thought about it for a while, and then I told him I'd go one time and see what it was like. Right away I met Matt. He is exactly my age. And he has a brother named Danny who sits for hours watching one scene from a video over and over and over again, just like Jonathan! We couldn't believe that our brothers did the very same thing. Or that we both have times when we feel down and sad about our brothers' problems. Matt said, "I love to fix things. I can fix lots of electronic stuff. Hey, I can fix almost anything. Anything except my brother's disability." He looked really down when he said that.

So I started telling him stories to cheer him up. Stories like the Fire Alarm Story and the Smoke Story. He laughed and told me some of his funny family stories. No one else but kids like us can under-

stand exactly how we feel. We live with it every day. We know how hard it is. And how sad it is, and how funny it is too. It's like we were picked as members of a club that we never asked to join.

On the other hand, talking with other siblings also makes me feel like I'm pretty lucky. Some kids have brothers or sisters who can't talk or can't move by themselves. Their bodies don't work well enough for them to walk, or run or skip or dance like Jonathan. Some of them can't play with their siblings. When they're thirsty or hungry, they can't tell someone. They can't talk to their siblings at all.

When I come home from a meeting, I'm nicer to Jonathan and I feel more glad that he is my brother. I'm also quieter for a while, because I need time to think. There are so many more kids like me than I ever knew.

# CHAPTER 13

# Maybe One Day

One day Mom was driving me to ballet class when we passed a billboard with a big picture of a TV star. "Do you see that man?" Mom pointed to the billboard. "Look at his eyes. What do you see?"

I looked. He was smiling, but with a real smile, not a fake Hollywood smile. "I don't know," I said. "It's kind of like his eyes are happy, but a little bit sad, too."

"Great observation," said Mom. "I've met him. He has a little girl with special needs."

"Does that make his eyes different?"

Mom laughed. "He's been through a lot," she said. "When his daughter was born and he found out that she was disabled, he felt so sad that he cried. Then he held her and he felt more love than he thought he could ever feel. Since then, she has brought him joy and all sorts of adventures he never would have had if she hadn't been disabled. I think his eyes show all those feelings."

I had to ask. "Does she also drive him crazy?"

"Yes!" Mom laughed again. "Definitely. All kids drive their parents crazy."

Whew! I slid down in my seat. It's always good to hear I'm not the only one. Mom must have read my thoughts, because she said, "He's a lot like you. When you get older, you'll realize what living with Jonathan has done for you, besides drive you crazy."

"Like what?" I said.

"You'll understand things that lots of other people don't understand, because they didn't have the challenge of living with a special needs sibling like you did.

"You'll be kinder and more patient with people, because living with Jonathan has tested you so much.

"Solving problems will be easier for you, because you've had a lot of practice.

"You already know what it feels like to be frustrated and upset with someone who can't change or who can't understand something that seems simple to you, so you'll know how to handle that kind of frustration.

"Maybe when someone comes to you feeling upset with another person, you'll know how to really listen. You'll know just how it feels."

I have a sneaky feeling that Mom's right. I guess one day I'll find out.

Meanwhile, I'll keep laughing.

I'll have special times with my parents.

I'll talk to people who really know how to listen.

I'll take a break.

I'll think like a genius.

I'll write and draw.

I'll be a kid.

And I'll dance.

I'll always dance.

# Resources

Computers and the internet make it possible to locate all kinds of resources in the blink of an eye. For example, to find current support groups for siblings of children with special needs, enter "sibling support groups AND special needs" or "sibling support groups special needs" into a web browser or search engine. For information and support regarding specific disabilities and disorders, enter the name of the disability or disorder. You should be able to find many groups and organizations dedicated to serving families living with a broad range of special needs. In the same way, you can find books and other materials from organization websites and on-line stores.

## MORE HELP FROM MAGINATION PRESS

Many Ways to Learn: Young People's Guide to Learning Disabilities
by Judith Stern and Uzi Ben-Ami, Ph.D.

Sparky's Excellent Misadventures: My ADD Journal, By Me (Sparky)
by Phyllis Carpenter and Marti Ford

Russell Is Extra Special: A Book About Autism for Children
by Charles A. Amenta III, M.D.

Sarah and Puffle: A Story for Children About Diabetes
by Linnea Mulder, R.N.

Learning to Slow Down and Pay Attention: A Book for Kids About ADD
by Kathleen Nadeau and Ellen Dixon

Putting on the Brakes: Young People's Guide to Understanding Attention Deficit Hyperactivity Disorder
by Patricia Quinn, M.D., and Judith Stern

The "Putting on the Brakes" Activity Book for Young People with ADHD
by Patricia Quinn, M.D., and Judith Stern

The Best of "Brakes"
by Patricia Quinn, M.D., and Judith Stern

Little Tree: A Story for Children with Serious Medical Problems
by Joyce C. Mills, Ph.D.

Breathe Easy: Young People's Guide to Asthma
by Jonathan H. Weiss, Ph.D.

Otto Learns About His Medicine: A Story About Medication for Children with ADHD
by Matthew Galvin, M.D.

Help Is on the Way: A Child's Book About ADD
by Marc A. Nemiroff, Ph.D., and Jane Annunziata, Psy.D.

What About Me? When Brothers and Sisters Get Sick
by Allan Peterkin, M.D.

You Can Call Me Willy: A Story for Children About AIDS
by Joan C. Verniero

### MAGINATION PRESS
750 First Street, NE, Washington, DC 20002, www.maginationpress.com

# About the Author

Natalie Hale is an author and illustrator whose books include *The Little Star's Journey: A Fairytale for Survivors of All Kinds*. The experience of teaching her son to read led to her founding Special Reads for Special Needs, a small press that produces picture books uniquely designed to make reading easier for children with special needs. She spends her days illustrating and producing these books under the watchful eyes of her cat, Zorro. She lives in Cincinnati, Ohio, with her family.

PHOTO BY REBECCA HALE

# About the Illustrator

Kate Sternberg grew up in western New York, where she graduated from Rochester Institute of Technology with a bachelor's degree in fine arts and a master's in art education. She is the author and illustrator of *Mama's Morning*, and has illustrated several other children's books, including *The Year My Mother Was Bald* and the Phoebe Flower's Adventures series. Kate is also an art teacher at Stone Middle School in Fairfax County, Virginia. Her family includes a husband, two sons, and assorted furry friends.

PHOTO BY REFLEXIONS